The Story of Crow

A
Nyul Nyul
Story

Written & Illustrated by Pat Torres.

yul Nyul Language Text by Magdalene Williams.

THE STORYTELLER

Magabala Books

P.O. Box 668, Broome,
West Australia. 6725.

Publishing venture of the Kimberley
Aboriginal Law & Culture Centre.
Supported by the National Aboriginal
& Torres Strait Islander Bicentennial Programme.

Book design by Schmitz Design (WA) Pty. Ltd.
Fun Map illustration by Merrilee Lands.
Printed by Em Complete Printers.
Perth, Western Australia.

National Library of Australia
Cataloguing - in - Publication Data:

The Story of Crow
for Children
ISBN 0 7316 7363.
(1) Aborigines, Australia — Torres, Pat, 1956– and Williams, Magdalene, 1921–

How To Speak in Nyul Nyul

SAY

a as the **u** in b**u**t
b as in **b**aby
d as in **d**ad
g as in **g**et but not as the g in giant
i as in **i**nk
j as in **j**ug
k as the **g** in hun**g**er or as the **k** in don**k**ey
l as in **l**et
ly as the **lli** in mi**lli**on but not as the ly in belly
m as in **m**an
n as in **n**et
o as in g**o**
oo as in m**oo**n
ng as in si**ng**
ny as the **ni** in o**ni**on but not as the ny in many
r as in **r**un but not as the r in car
rd as an American says the **rd** in ca**rd**
rl as an American says the **rl** in Ca**rl**
rn as an American says the **rn** in ba**rn**
rr as the **r**'s in p**rrr** like a cat purring
w as in **w**ind
y as in **y**et.

Jooyi nyimoongk jabal,
Wangkid jinijirr jabal yoomboon Waragayir.

I wonder if

you know,

The story

of the Crow?

Wangkid jinijirr moongkan boolgarr,
Arri mangka ngaliyirr.

His feathers once
were white,

Not black
and charcoal bright.

Gawoogaj nooloo layibinyirr liyan,
Banangkarr Wangkid ibagarndin riyib niman

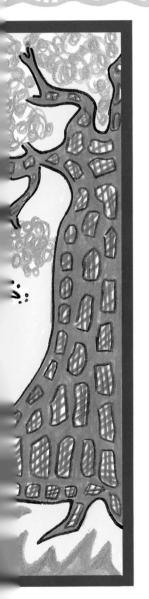

He sang a song
 so full of joy, they say,

Not like the croaking voice
 he has today.

Boogarrigarr Wangkid layinybird inyoorr
Waragayin jinijirr winjid, Wangkid jibirr ibagarr

In Dreamtime
he stole the Eagle's wife,

And that's what
brought him strife.

Waragayin bilijindin jinijirr winjid, Waragayir wayinjid boogarri jinijirr winjida Wangkid.

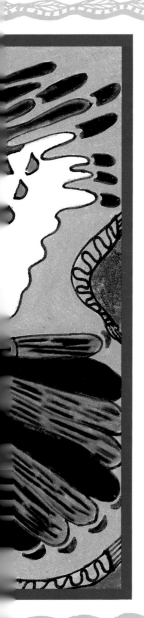

When the angry husband

soaring high, spied the two,

He thought about

what he would do.

Waragayin wayinjid inyoorr marl rrik.

The Eagle swooped down
to the ground,

And grasped a burning coal
that he had found.

Waragayin wayinjid injibinjibin Wangkid, Riyib Wangkid.

Then he searched
both high and low,

To find the handsome
but naughty Crow.

18

When all at once he saw
the crow singing below!

The Eagle flew up high
to drop the coal all a-glow.

Wangkid jinijirr nimanj ingkamarr, Windijin wambrinj Wangkid ibagarndin riyib mangag

20

Inside his throat
the colour red,

Shows the world the burning
coal that Crow was fed.

Banangkarr Wangkid ibagarndin mangk moongkan.

22

Today he's burnt

right through,

To show the world

what they shouldn't do.

Arriban milij,
Mibiganda janijarr mijid layib magara.

24

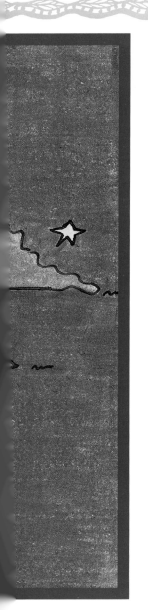

So keep the laws,
   don't mess around,

Don't put yourself
   on sacred ground.

Nyul Nyul Meanings

Arri	Not.	Jabal
Arriban	Don't.	Janijarr
		Jibin
Babaningwarr	Children.	Jibirr
Banangkar	Today.	Jinijirr
Bilijindin	Became angry/	Joorrgor
	got wild.	Jooyi
Boogarri	To dream/think	
	about.	Gadagor
Boogarrigarr	Dreamtime.	Gawoog
Boolgarr	White.	
		Layib
Ibagarndin	To have.	Layibinyi
Imbanj	Finish now.	Layinbir
Ingkamarr	Burnt.	Liyan
Inijal	He saw.	
Iningoorl	He threw/	Magara
	dropped.	Mangag
Injibinjibin	To look for.	Mangk
Inyoorr	To take away.	Mangka
		Mibigan
		Milij
		Moongk

26

ory.	Ngaliyirr	Shining/bright.
ur people.	Ngalook	The White Cockatoo.
to.		
d luck.	Nimanj	Throat/voice.
longing to/his.	Nooloo	Corroborree songs.
oodbye.		
.	Nyimoongk	You know.
verything.	Riyib	Bad luck.
nging.	Rrik	Coal.
ght.	Wambrinj	People.
ood.	Wangkawang	All of a sudden.
steal.	Wangkid	The Crow.
elings.	Waragayin	The Eagle.
	Wayinjid	Went.
ad/path.	Wilirrminy	The Blue Mountain Parrot (Eagle's wife).
rever.		
ck.		
ck and.	Windijin	To tell.
ep.	Winjid	Wife.
that.	Winjida	Wife and.
ather/hair.		

The Story of Crow

I wonder if you know,
The story of the Crow?

His feathers once were white,
Not black and charcoal bright.

He sang a song so full of joy, they say,
Not like the croaking voice he has today.

In Dreamtime he stole the Eagle's wife
And that's what brought him strife.

When the angry husband soaring high, spied the
He thought about what he would do.

The Eagle swooped down to the ground,
And grasped a burning coal that he had found.

Then he searched both high and low,
To find the handsome but naughty Crow.

When all at once he saw the crow singing belov
The Eagle flew up high to drop the coal all a-glc

Inside his throat the colour red,
Shows the world the burning coal that Crow was

Today he's burnt right through,
To show the world what they shouldn't do.

So keep the laws, don't mess around,
Don't put yourself on sacred ground.

Wangkid Jinijirr Jabal

yi nyimoongk jabal,
ngkid jinijirr jabal yoomboon Waragayin?

ngkid jinijirr moongkan boolgarr,
mangka ngaliyirr.

woogaj nooloo layibinyirr liyan,
angkarr Wangkid ibagarndin riyib nimanj.

garrigarr Wangkid layinybird inyoorr Waragayin jinijirr winjid,
ngkid jibirr ibagarndin.

ragayin bilijindin jinijirr winjid,
ragayin wayinjid boogarri jinijirr winjida Wangkid.

ragayin wayinjid inyoorr marl rrik.

ragayin wayinjid injibinjibin Wangkid,
Wangkid.

ngkawang inijal Wangkid,
oorl marl rrik jimbin Wangkid jinijirr nimanj.

ngkid jinijirr nimanj ingkamarr,
dijin wambrinj Wangkid ibagarndin riyib mangagarr.

angkarr Wangkid ibagarndin mangk moongkan.

an milij,
ganda janijarr mijid layib magara.

Ngarlan

Ngarlan
is where the
Nyul Nyul
People live.

Gadagor imbanj wambrinj.

All is finished now people.